Gwyneth

Growing Up in the Mountains of North Wales During **WWII**

Audrey A. Duncan

Knoxville, Tennessee, United States of America
https://www.crippledbeaglepublishing.com/home

Cover Design: Loysa de los Angeles
Artist: Jolene Scheepers

ISBN for Hardcover: 978-1-965334-99-7
ISBN for paperback: 978-1-965334-50-8

Printed in the United States of America.

Gwyneth

Growing Up in the Mountains
of North Wales
During **WWII**

Audrey A. Duncan

Hiriarth

We'll keep a welcome in the hillside
We'll keep a welcome in the vale
This land will still be waiting
When you come home again to Wales

Gwyneth was born in the mountains of North Wales during the time of World War ll. Although there was no invasion of the mountains, the effects of the war surrounded her in many ways. Her father had a mountain sheep farm, as did his brother over the next hill and his father over yonder. There were hundreds and hundreds of sheep, and to Gwyneth, her whole world was centered around sheep. She did not know of a life without sheep.

She lived in an old gray stone house, called Bryn Mawr, with a gray slate roof; it gave the appearance of a stone hill blending into the green pastures surrounding it before stretching upward to the moorlands above. The moorland consisted of a sturdy mossy grass that the sheep loved, but there were also gorse bushes, with lovely yellow blossoms in the summer; many groves of purple heather; and much bracken (tall ferns) and rhododendron, beautiful to look at but called by the farmers "the Himalayan weed." Brought in from India by the gentry to their estates in the Empire days, rhododenron was very invasive and often set afire, as it choked out the grass needed for the grazing sheep. There was nothing more beautiful than the moorland in summer though.

In those days, sharing the moorland with the sheep were herds of wild ponies that frolicked on the hills, adding an array of colors, from black, white, and brown to pinto. They would form clans of their own as the stallions tried to gather the females to form their own families. If there was one thing that Gwyneth loved more than sheep, it was those mountain ponies, and she finally persuaded her father to catch two white ones and tame, or "break," them, as it was called. They became "Twilight" and "Twinkles" and were part of her life for quite a few years, galloping the hills to entering and winning many gymkhanas and pony dressage blue ribbons.

Now, Gwyneth wasn't an only child; she had a brother named Mordecai (he was called Mort). He was a true Welshman with short, black hair and a fiery disposition. Two years older than his sister, he was the leader and the one who got into trouble over his various antics. When he was about ten or so, he had become quite well known in the local village for his mischievous behavior. The village held concerts periodically in the village hall, and Mort, having a beautiful descant voice, broke the crowd into laughter when he sang "I want to be like Jesus."

He and Gwyneth had quite different preferences for entertainment, she with her ponies and two white angora rabbits that her mother had bought her for her birthday. She once decided to bathe them, and her mother came in to find her drying them by the fire. That was the first and last time. The rabbits lived in pens near the house, but Gwyneth would let them out to run around the front lawn much to the consternation of Old Tom, the outdoor cat. Well, all the cats lived outdoors, in the barns, to catch mice or rats and were given milk only at milking time. No cats or dogs were allowed in the house; they were working animals.

Old Tom was a good rabbit catcher, but he did not see the angora rabbits as regular rabbits; they would run up to him if he crossed the lawn. His hair would rise on the back of his neck in horror as he ran away. Mort liked whippets (small greyhounds) and ferrets. He would put a leash on the ferrets and send them down rabbit holes to catch rabbits, and the whippets, which likewise loved to catch rabbits, could chase them in the open fields, and being great runners, would often run them down. Rabbits would zigzag, but whippets knew this and would keep a straight run until they collided.

The farmyard and barns were great sources of entertainment, like playgrounds for today's children. The bumpy stone yard was large, with the house on one side and a field with a pond on another side and an offshoot lane going down to the barns. It was the place for the wanderers, hens picking up seeds or whatever, and ducks and geese heading to and from the pond.

They all supplied food for the family—eggs from the hens and roasted chickens, roasted duck, rich eggs for cake making, and roasted goose for Christmas dinner or other special meals. Well, Mort and the gander were at odds for many a year, and although he denied it, Mort had a catapult and would, given the chance, shoot pebbles at the gander. The result was that the gander was forever chasing both Gwyneth and Mort with flapping wings, and if they were not fast enough, they got a good peck on their bottoms.

The barns were seventh heaven for Gwyneth and Mort with lofts to climb into to play hide-and-seek, stalls for the two cart horses, and of course, smaller ones for the ponies. Other barns were for milking cows; milk was mainly for home consumption and the making of butter and wonderful cream trifles. There were barns full of stored hay for winter feeding, along with bins of grain. The barn that attracted much attention was the cow barn.

When milking began on a twice-daily routine, the cats and dogs came in for special treats of warm milk from bowls located nearby. Sometimes the milkers would squeeze a teat in the direction of a cat or dog; they would bounce to see if they could catch the squirt in their mouth, and sometimes there would be bouncing children too. There never seemed to be any animosity between the cats and dogs. They knew that they all lived there together and that they had a purpose in life. If it was a harsh winter, of which there were many in the 1930s and 1940s, these barns were busy places, for most animals were brought in.

Not the sheep, of course, because there were too many. However, the life of most sheep was a short one, for they were raised for meat and wool. Lambs are born in the spring, usually in the lower pastures. The sheep are up on the moors for summer; brought back to the pastures in the autumn for shearing, dipping (to kill the parasites), and branding; then many go to market before winter.

The hill farmers would walk them down to the nearest market town for sheep sales. The prize rams and the breeding ewes and the best of the crop were kept as the basic stock. If the winter was harsh or the ewe had birthing problems and she died, there would often be orphan lambs. They were brought to the barns, and then everyone was kept busy feeding them until they were weaned.

Gwyneth and Mort were big-time lamb feeders, filling bottles of milk, attaching a rubber teat to the bottle, and feeding the lambs. Both humans and lambs enjoyed this activity, which went on for several weeks.

However, something unusual happened that changed the game: The lambs grew faster than Gwyneth and Mort, and because weaning time meant stretching the feeding times out, the lambs would follow them around and bump them looking for their meal. It became a whole new ball game to flee the growing lambs.

When Mort was almost six and Gwyneth was four, they started going to school, early for her and a little late for him (due to the regulation of the school system; it depended on the actual date of birth), at the village of Llanfyhangel y Mochnant. The school was close to a mile away, so their father, T. J., would take them on his motorcycle, which had a sidecar attached to it. There was room for the two on the sidecar seat, but if it was raining, they would race to see who could get down into the pointed nose of the sidecar first, where it was warm and dry.

Many children walked to school, as the school bus was in the future. It was a new school, run by the state, which replaced the church school, still there but now used for church and village functions. In the 1930 to 1940 era, classes were held in English, for Welsh and Gaelic (old Celtic languages) were in the decline because people realized that they had to be bilingual to be equal to their English neighbors in employment and the like. By the twentieth century, both languages were offered as second languages, as they realized the value of preserving them.

Gwyneth never could understand why her father had three surnames—Thomas James Lewis—instead of having a Christian name or two followed by a surname. They had to explain to her that Thomas, James, or Lewis could be either one. Generally, he was called Daddy to her, T. J. to his friends, and Mr. Lewis (pronounced Lowis in Welsh) to everyone else.

SCHOOL

LLANFAIRPWLLGWYNGYLL
GOGERYCHWYRNDROBWLLLLANTYSILIOGOGOH

Being bilingual, there were many things that had to be sorted out in Gwyneth's mind concerning the names of people and towns in Welsh that didn't apply if translated to English. Many men had the same Christian name in Wales, like Idris or Rhys. So in a small village, to differentiate, they would add his occupation to his name, saying Idris grocer or Idris post office.

Many towns and villages use the word llan (town) in front of them, like Llangadfan or Llanfyllin, or a descriptive name, like Bryn Mawr and Bryn Fach, meaning large hill and little hill. Thus, as a child, Gwyneth had to learn where to put that adjective—small hill or hill small.

The ultimate name for a little village is in Anglesey, North Wales, named Llanfairpwllgwyngyllgogerychwyrndrobwllllantysiliogogogoch.

It is pronounced llan-fair-pwll-gwyn-gyll-go-ger-ych-wyrn-drob-wll-llan-ty-silio-go-go-goch. Roughly speaking, it means "St. Mary's Church in the hollow of the white hazel near to the fierce whirlpool of St. Tysilio of the red cave," and at the railway station, its sign goes from one end of the platform to the other.

The Welsh call it Llanfair PG! Due to the many rivers in Wales with the mountains carrying the waters down to the sea on three sides of the country, many towns and villages begin with the word aber, which means estuary, so we have Aberystwyth and Aberdovey, meaning the mouth of the river Ystwyth and the river Dovey.

In the village, there was quite an assortment of churches and chapels—the Church of England, the Calvinistic Methodist Chapel, the Wesleyan Chapel, and the Baptist Chapel—so there was ample choice for this rural area. The Church of England was sparsely attended, but the chapels were full. And the village resounded with singing in the two pubs on Saturday night as people got ready for chapel singing on Sunday, for the Welsh love to sing.

Most Welsh villages had a male choir, and they would compete with each other at the National Eisteddfod singing event or poetry competition to take home the cup for singing or become the bard of the year for poetry. This event alternated between North and South Wales annually. Gwyneth's mother was a member of the Church of England, and her father was a Methodist. It didn't produce many problems; they grew up in these churches, so they stayed with their own church when married.

Hence, Gwyneth and Mort attended both places of worship and were confirmed in the church and made members of the chapel. The usual routine was that once a month her mother would go to 8:00 a.m. communion at the church on her own; then every Sunday, the children would go to the 11:00 church service with her, home for Sunday dinner, to chapel for Sunday school at 2:00 p.m., home for tea, and to chapel with their father at 6:00 p.m.

Sunday was an exciting time for the children, for they enjoyed all of these activities. Somewhere in all this religion, Gwyneth was faced with the statement that "God is watching you," probably when she was misbehaving, which led her on a major project—she started to look for God: "Where was he watching her that she couldn't see him?"

At church she looked around all the pillars that lined the aisles, and up at the altar, and behind the organ. At Sunday school, she even had others help, but the evening chapel finally got her into trouble, as she was under the seat several times and just couldn't sit still while looking.

Finally, her father said, "What is the matter?" and she told him that she was looking for God. Angrily he said, "If you don't stop, the Lord, the devil, and me will make an appearance, and you will have a bottom spanking from all three."

After supper that night, Daddy and she had a little talk about the invisible God. Gwyneth nodded her head when he asked if she understood, but nevertheless, she still looked around cautiously when she was up to a little mischief.

Gwyneth loved her family. They were her life—her Mummy and Daddy and brother, Mort; all of her father's family, his brother, wife, and daughter at the next farm; and her grandparents too, who lived quite close at the Rhos. Her aunt, or father's sister Amelia, lived with them and took care of her grandmother, who had the Spanish flu during WWII, which resulted in her getting Parkinson's disease. Gwyneth and Mort would sometimes cross the hills to visit them, and one time, they were caught in a thunderstorm, which blew Gwyneth's umbrella inside out. She cried, for it was a prized possession of hers.

Her mother was one of thirteen and had grown up on another farm, Garth Fach, and nine of her brothers went off to America after WWI to a Welsh settlement in the Rochester and Utica, New York, area.

The three girls and one boy stayed home. I will tell Gwyneth's mother's adventurous story in a while. One sister had six children and the other had four, but none lived on a farm; hence, things were much harder for them during the early and mid-thirties. So much so that every summer when school was out, they would be brought up to Bryn Mawr to stay on the farm, where food and fun were plentiful. What a time they had sharing the life of Gwyneth and Mort, sleeping in the lofts in the stables and frolicking in the mountains of Wales.

Two things gradually led to a more prosperous life for the farmer. As the 1930s came to a close, the world recovered from the Great Depression, and as the war became more and more imminent, Britain saw the need to produce more of its own food. Farming became very important, particularly the production of meats and grains. Farmers made money, old Dobbin retired by selling Massey Harris tractors, double-daylight saving time was introduced to give them longer daylight hours to work the land, and Gwyneth's whole world vastly changed overnight. The young men went off to war. The farm owners were kept in place, but their sons were replaced by Land Girls, women who came out from the cities to work on the land and turned the fields into massive market gardens. They were housed in the villages or on the farms and caused quite a sensation in their snazzy plus-four uniforms.

As the bombing increased in the cities, the parents began to send their children to the villages in the country. Near Gwyneth's village, there were four great halls in the surrounding valleys, and the owners turned them over to house the children. They had matrons to take care of them, and they were added to the schools. They came in crocodile lines each morning, and the local children were admonished to make them welcome. What an adjustment that was for all. First, it was the accents. When strong Welsh accents struggled to understand the Liverpudlian accents, laughter ensued.

As most of the evacuees to this area were from the bombed-out dock areas of Liverpool and Birkenhead, they came from the very poor areas, bringing with them head lice, scabies, and such diseases. For a time, these spread to the local children until the locals were able to clean things up. It didn't take long for the local children to realize that these were city kids who didn't know a thing about rural life, so a little fun and teasing issued. One of the favorite jokes was to give them each a penny and send them to the local grocery store for a pint of pigeon's milk, saying it was really delicious. Of course, the grocer soon realized what was happening to them; so instead, he would give them a licorice stick for their penny. They were scared of the cows, particularly if they met the herd coming down the road for milking and would run back to the schoolyard screaming. In time, the two groups began to play together, and it was like having another family. Although previously warned by her parents not to let the new children ride the ponies (Gwyneth and Mort were riding them to school now), Gwyneth did, and alas, a little girl fell off and broke her clavicle. Gwyneth was grounded for some weeks following that incident.

As the war progressed, there were other changes in the valleys. Quonset huts were erected, and tents were put up on the fields in the valleys, as the country had to create prisoner-of-war camps. One group was for Germans, another for Italians, and another for Polish women and children whose husbands had come over and joined the British Army.

GROCER

The prisoners were kept in the camps at first, but as the Allies progressed and the outcome of the war looked more definite, both the Germans and the Italians were allowed to work on the farms. This revealed an interesting fact: that the farmers soon wanted Germans rather than Italians, the reason being that the Germans were just naturally hard workers whatever the task, whereas the Italians would prefer to sit under the trees and sing or whistle at the Land Girls!

The Polish women were of course free to walk around the valley, and many took up dressmaking for the locals to make a little money. As Gwyneth looked back in later years, she remembered a peculiar incident concerning the Polish families. Even though their husbands were fighting with the Allies, they were all Catholic, and a bus would take them monthly to the nearest town for them to attend Mass. Petrol was rationed and extremely scarce, and the locals resented this small favor. Somehow, Gwyneth knew that this was not right.

Petrol was rationed and was indeed very scarce, so trips to nearby towns were not possible. However, by this time, Gwyneth's father had extended his farming to a trucking business to take the farmers' stock and field crops to the cities, where food was needed. This led to an exciting addition to Gwyneth's life. Parts would break down on the tractors or lorries, and Gwyneth and her mother would be sent off to town to purchase the part.

By this time, her mother was driving a little Austin car. This meant they could obtain the equipment for the tractor or whatever and could have a look or two in the shops, but most of all, it meant they could go to the pictures, a great treat to enjoy, particularly because the little usherette would come through with ice cream cups or even have a Cadbury chocolate bar.

Well, one time a disaster overtook them on the way home. It was already dark, so they had the dim lights on, which gave just a little light aimed at the ground. They didn't know if the pilot saw the lights or if he was just unloading a bomb. The planes came after dark to Liverpool and the docks and bombed them; if they had not dropped all their bombs before the guns became too fierce, they would return home over the Welsh hills and drop their cargo anywhere to lighten their load so they could make it back to Germany.

At any rate, one pilot dropped a bomb, which hit the road just in front of the car and threw the car up in the air and headfirst into the roadside ditch. Both Gwyneth and her mother cried and then hugged each other. They didn't appear to be worse for the crash. They climbed out of the car, which was quite a struggle given its position, and walked across the field to a nearby farm. The farmer got off his tractor, and they all went across the fields to the car, which he was able to pull out and take back across the fields to the farm. There would be no driving on the road until they filled in that hole. By that time, Gwyneth's father had arrived in his old army jeep, concerned by the fact that they were so late. They exchanged hugs and kisses, and then they went home on the other side of the bomb hole.

Food was obtained with ration books, which allotted each person a certain amount of food per month. This included meat, fish, poultry, and all the staples. Now, the Lewis family and others who worked the land did not feel the pinch as much as others, although they were accounted for, as inspectors came and counted sheep and all the other livestock. Everyone, even those in the cities, had a victory garden, where they grew their own vegetables and raised a chicken or two. Bryn Mawr had an orchard of apples, pears, plums and canes of raspberries, black and red currants, and of course gooseberries. Who could live without gooseberry pie? Rarities were oranges or citrus fruits of any kind, grapes and bananas, and anything tropical. One time, when they did get bananas, Mort told Gwyneth that you needed to eat the whole thing (although he knew better), and when her mother came in, Gwyneth was sick from having eaten a banana, skin and all.

Humans adapt to their situations, and during the war this went on big time as they took up the swapping game. The river Vyrnwy was nearby and, like many Welsh rivers, was flush with salmon and trout. The farmers or landowners who owned the part of the river on their land would rent out stretches of the river to city folk or well-to-dos for the fishing rights, and they would come in their free time to fish. The villagers took to gaffing at night where they could catch salmon and trout easily with the aid of a strong flashlight and a bobby who chose to ignore such activities. They could gaff the fish because they were attracted to the light. The locals enjoyed many a juicy fish dinner.

Another alternative was the swap game with a farmer, a salmon or two for a flitch of bacon or a nice fat goose. This same rule applied to the hill country. Outsiders would rent parcels of land for grouse or pheasant shooting during the season, but the locals caught these birds for eating or trading them. Gwyneth's mother, a fine driver, would spot a covey of pheasants on the road, drive slowly, and then with a quick spurt as the pheasants rose, catch several with a small bump to stun them but not enough to annihilate them. Rabbits were a good source of meat for all country people. Both Gwyneth and Mort knew how to skin a rabbit and cut it into pieces, preserving the parts on either side of the spine as the choice pieces. The rabbit was then covered with strips of bacon and roasted in the oven.

Cows, pigs, and sheep were more or less under the control of the national inspectors, as they kept good counts. Another source of food came from the gypsies, who traveled around the country in horse-drawn caravans with small herds of goats. They would park their caravans on the commons (free land) and stay awhile to sell goat meat, cheese, and nonfood items such as baskets, rugs, pots, and pans. Other nomads were the Spanish onion men, who would arrive on the farms with big Spanish onions on ropes to sell alongside offers to help bring in the harvest for a few meals and a pound or two.

Then there was the Home Guard. Each community and its surrounding farms had to have a Home Guard unit. Their purpose in the countryside was to look for spies, or infiltrators who were seeking ways to sabotage the country. The Home Guard was composed mainly of the too young, too old, or exempt men. They had uniforms and trained weekly (when possible). Gwyneth's father was in the Home Guard, although he resented it due to his heavy workload. The Home Guard was run by an old colonel from WWI who was a stickler for following rules and regulations. So they marched and practiced maneuvers whenever he could get a handful of people together.

One time, when Daddy came home with his rifle, the children wanted him to march around the parlor, which he did to amuse them. Unfortunately, he hit the chandelier with his bayonet, and the whole thing came crashing down. They spent the rest of the war with a single bulb in the parlor, for there were no replacements. Another time, a man was seen on top of Dyffryn hill, and the whole Home Guard was called out to find him. They did eventually, but he turned out to be a hiker looking for signs of an Iron Age fort on the summit of the hill. In the cities and the bombed-out areas, the Home Guard played a very important part in assisting the people but were not quite as necessary up in the hills of Wales.

However, after the horrors of WWI, there was a great fear of gas, so everyone was issued a gas mask, even the children and the elderly. Gwyneth had one. It was enclosed in a small mask that had a strap so that she could wear it around her neck to school and most other places. Well, not around the farm. Children soon found out that you could unscrew the bottom of the mask and that it was a grand place to carry conkers, which are the big nuts found in the fruit of horse chestnuts and a grand object for a game. When you take the nut out of its big green shell, this reveals a big brown nut. You then hammer a nail through its center with a long string attached and tie a knot onto the end of the string, and you have a target for war. Playing Sir Lancelot and Sir Galahad, you would hold the string at one end and toss the bullet (nut) at your opponent's bullet, which was tossed at the same time. The goal was to see who could split the other's nut first and be declared the winner.

To the east of North Wales were the flat lowlands of the Shropshire plains, which were clearly visible from the mountains of Wales. It was here that many of the big air bases were located, both British and American, where they trained before moving over to bases in East Anglia and such on the eastern coast of England. They were for the most part practice sites for the bombers and the fighters. They would roar up the Welsh valleys, rapidly descending before making a sharp turn into the next valley.

GAS MASK

Troops would train in the mountains, too, so it became quite a contrast from the usual calm and peaceful mountains. One day, two American cousins, sons of the brothers from Utica, arrived at Bryn Mawr. There was much excitement and chatter upon their arrival. Because they were based in Shropshire, they received many visits, as well as chewing gum, chocolates, tins of corned beef, and 15 denier nylons, a lovely switch for Gwyneth's mother from lyle hose.

Now, Gwyneth's mother's sister, Megan, the one with eight children, had a husband who was a pianist. He never did make much money playing piano, but during the war, he got a job running the bar and providing the entertainment at one of the American bases near Shrewsbury. Somehow (we don't know quite how), he made lots of money, so much that by the end of the war, he was able to buy the Wingfield Arms Hotel near Shrewsbury. The children got good schooling, and one of Gwyneth's close cousins married a lawyer who became a barrister and went into politics. Ultimately he was knighted.

Another sister, Myvanwy, the baby of thirteen, stayed at home with her parents at Garth Fach and during the war, met a British officer on one of the Shropshire bases. They were engaged for several years, only for her to find out that he was already married and had a family down in Dover. Myvanwy then decided to visit her American brothers. She married in Utica, divorced in Utica, and returned to Wales but later went back to America, where she stayed until she died. Each ocean crossing was made with two China spaniels, which used to sit on either end of the mantelpiece wherever she lived, and the relatives used to tease her about these well-traveled dogs.

The third sister married a painter, a regular paint-your-house painter, who got his start by painting the wrought iron railing all the way around Lake Vyrnwy, a reservoir for Liverpool located in the hills of Wales. Through trial and error, he eventually set up as an interior decorator, had an affair and a baby with his assistant, and divorced his wife, Rhiannon. Upon hearing the news, Rhiannon started throwing their Royal Dalton China at him and around the dining room until it all ended up in pieces on the floor. There was no news as to how many actually hit the husband, Harry.

The village hall is where the Women's Institute ladies met to do their projects. During the war, knitting was the thing—khaki-colored scarves, toboggans, gloves, and socks for their brave men at war. Gwyneth became quite adept at turning the heel of socks with four needles instead of the usual two. There were items to be sewn also, like the heavy black curtains for every household in the village and the farms so that not a speck of light could be seen from the skies when the bombers came over. There were wardens who checked each area at dusk. There were several Singer treadle sewing machines in the hall for the purpose of making these drapes, and great care had to be taken with these old machines because if the needle broke, it was not replaceable.

PORCES
W I
CONCERT

There was fun to be had in the village hall too. Folks gathered in the evening to play whist (forerunner of bridge) and to have concerts. Another pastime was the telling of tales, many true, but some with perhaps a pinch of salt added. I will relate one of Gwyneth's favorite stories, perhaps because she knew the characters. The village lay on either side of the main road that passed straight through it, with smaller roads leading off each side. Starting at one end was the police station (the bobby did his rounds on his bicycle), followed by some cottages intermingled between the institute, the church, and the churchyard. Then there were three chapels, two pubs, a grocery store, a butcher, the post office, a few tall houses, and a very small bank, all of which ended at the other end with a petrol station.

Now, down near the police station, in one of the cottages lived Ellen Roberts, a well-respected spinster whom everyone knew for her many good deeds. Through the years, she was someone who could be counted on to lend a hand, whether it be cooking for the sick, knitting, arranging flowers in the church, or babysitting little Johnny. The village became aware that Miss Roberts would become a centenarian (one hundred years old) that coming summer, and the village elders—the vicar, the banker, the schoolteacher, and a few others—got together to discuss the possibility of doing something to celebrate her birthday. Because they didn't know quite what a centenarian would like, they decided to visit her to ask. They knocked on her door, which was a double-gated affair, where you could open just the top of the door.

Miss Roberts appeared, smiling and rubbing her hands together, as was her custom, and said, "Oh, how nice. To what do I owe this pleasure?" The vicar explained the purpose for their visit and asked her how she would like to celebrate her birthday. Quite flustered now, she said, "Oh, I don't really think that I need anything," but the group persisted, saying that there must be something that they could do for her. She stood there for awhile, still rubbing those long sinewy hands together, and finally said, "Well, you know for years now, I have had this dream that one day I would like to run from one end of the village to the other in the altogether." Well, of course, the men were flabbergasted. "Oh dear," said the vicar, "you are of course joking." "Not at all," she replied. "You asked what I would like to do and that is my reply."

This was followed by some discussion by the committee, and they finally said that it would be possible if she would do it early in the morning before the villagers were up and about and she would start up by the petrol station and end up at the police station, where she could dress again. They chose the following Wednesday at 6:00 a.m.

The day of the event, Ellen Roberts came out of her cottage in the altogether, turned left, and headed up to the petrol station going at a fair clip for her age. However, there was something that the organizers had forgotten. It was market day in Oswestry, and the bus from Llanfair passed through Llanfihangel at an early hour to pick up passengers who were taking their produce to market. Two old-timers, Alan Thomas and Dai Griffiths, always came out early and sat on the bench outside the bank to see who was getting on the bus and what they were taking to sell. Well, the bus came and went on its early schedule, a few passengers had left with it, and now Alan and Dai continued to sit to contemplate the world in general.

Suddenly, they noticed a figure coming toward them at a fair clip, and then swish! It had gone by. "Who was that?" asked Dai. "I don't know," said Alan. "He or she went by too fast." A few minutes later, that person came round the corner in the opposite direction, and they had a better look. "Well, I do believe that was Miss Ellen Roberts running by," said Alan. "I think so too," said Dai, "but whatever was she wearing?" "I don't know," said Alan, "but whatever it was, it certainly needed ironing."

RED D
NN

As well as these humorous stories, there were scary tales that the children loved. Once again, we go to Dyffryn hill. Near the summit was a long ridge, which probably was a defense wall for the Iron Age fort that many visited. But another story was that it was a giant's grave and if you walked up and down on it seven times, the giant would turn over in his grave! Of course, the children always did it only six times. On another hillside, there was a pool, Llyndy pool, and one time, when a man disappeared and they couldn't find him, they decided to drag the mirky pool. They found the man, but when they pulled him out, he was full of holes, like a hunk of Swiss cheese, where giant eels had been going through him.

Then another time, a village man who had gone to America many years ago left a request in his will that his ashes be sent back and scattered on this famous Dyffryn hill. The vicar, Gwyneth's father, and a gathering of the locals climbed the hill, and when the vicar gave the order, Daddy was to scatter the ashes over the hill. Unfortunately, it was a windy day, and the ashes covered the vicar and everyone else up there. The vicar said it was far too windy in Wales to have future burials in this manner.

One more thing about Dyffryn hill—it provided two spectacular events, one of terror, as they could see Liverpool on fire during the night raids, and one of awe, as they could watch the northern lights.

Gwyneth's love for so many contributed to her happy youth, and her great love for one person was complete adoration. She loved her beyond comprehension, and the love was mutual. It was, of course, her mother (Mummy to Gwyneth), Margaret Louisa Lewis, known as Louie or Sister. Her children were the reason for her being. This said, however, Louie was a woman before her time, a woman who from the beginning knew that she wanted something different from that of her mother, who had raised thirteen children on a small farm in the mountains during a worldwide war followed by a worldwide depression.

Louie's mother had seen nine of her sons leave together for America to go to a Welsh settlement near the Utica and Rochester area in New York, never to see them again. Louie struggled to know how to change. When she and her brother, Ernest (known as Ernie), left school at about fifteen or sixteen years old, they decided to visit their brothers in America. They worked on the farm and other farms to earn enough money to buy steerage tickets from Bristol to New York, where they were met by some of their uncles at Ellis Island.

They spent the next two years with them. Ernie worked for the brothers and Louie worked as a nanny in Rochester, New York. She was delighted to be taken to Florida during the severe winters, the likes of which they had never seen in Wales. Both were about eighteen, and after much discussion, they decided that their hiraeth (longing) for Wales was too strong for them to remain away forever. Ernie obtained a small holding to farm in Wales, and fast-forward a few years, he was able to buy Dolobran Hall, with a large acreage where he raised Holstein Friesian (black-and-white) cattle and showed them at the agricultural fairs until he became a judge. Dolobran Hall was an old Quaker establishment under the National Trust; so although they owned it, no alteration could be made without the trust's permission. There is a tunnel that goes from the hall to the woods where the Quakers used to meet. Today, it is owned by Lloyd's of London, descendants of the Quakers.

Mummy, or Louie, visited awhile in Wales but then was off to London to attend nursing school at Guy's Hospital for the next three years. Near the East End of London, she worked in the poor area as an intern and delivered many babies. Graduating in her early twenties, she pondered about what to do next, and eventually decided to return to Wales, of course. She was able to get a position as a district nurse in the area where all her relatives lived and got lodging at a farm near the Rhos. Her first purchase was a horse, which the doctors and the preachers also used for travel.

Because it was too hilly for a bicycle, she progressed to a motorbike and finally, a car. She wore a uniform that included a veil and was called Sister Woods, for the nurses had developed through the church. Well, what happened was she met Gwyneth's father-to-be when she attended his mother, who had Parkinson's disease, and so began the romance. They married and moved to their new home at Bryn Mawr.

You would think that Louise would now settle down as the farmer's wife, Mrs. Thomas James Lewis, but no. That was not what she wanted to do. When the children were born, she hired two maids/nannies, Dot and Eva, to take care of the house and the children so that she could continue as a district nurse and, later, a health visitor and, finally, an area nursing director.

The raging war gradually abated as the 1940s progressed, and the evacuees went back to their parents, the Land Girls went back to the cities, the prisoners of war went home, the Polish refugees were united with their families, and the air bases on the Shropshire plains were dismantled. A few of the intruders were to stay forever, blending into the Welsh villages with a store or two or marrying a farmer's daughter. Was the peace and calm restored to the mountains of Wales? To a certain extent, but it never again would see the tranquility of Gwyneth's youth.

Gwyneth's life went through a complete metamorphosis, for she went away to a boarding school, followed by much travel and ultimately a life abroad. She experienced a wonderful and happy life, but within her was always a longing, a hiraeth, for her native Wales. She would lie awake at night envisioning riding a pony over the glorious hills of Wales and breathing in the scent of the yellow gorse and the purple heather of the moorlands.

We'll keep a welcome in the hillsides
We'll keep a welcome in the vales
This land you knew will still be singing
When you come home again to Wales.

Images from Audrey's life

Figure 1 Audrey

Figure 2 Audrey

Figure 3 Audrey and her cousin Rhoda

Figure 4 Audrey's brother Horace Mordecai (Mort) at 2 years old

Figure 5 Audrey's brother Mort

Figure 6 Mort on a pig

Figure 7 Mort

Figure 8 Audrey's father, Audrey, and Audrey's brother

Figure 9 Thomas James Lewis (Audrey's father) - 5 years old

Figure 10 Audrey's father Thomas James Lewis

Figure 11 Audrey's father and their horse

Figure 12 Thomas James Lewis and Audrey

Figure 13 Margaret Louisa Wood (Audrey's mother)

Figure 14 Audrey's mother, Audrey, and Audrey's cousin Rhoda

Figure 15 Audrey's uncle Thomas Wood (mother's side)

Figure 16 Audrey's father, mother, and grandfather

Figure 17 Grandpa Wood (Audrey's maternal grandfather)

Figure 18 Grandma Wood (Audrey's maternal grandmother)

Figure 19 Grandpa Lewis (Audrey's paternal grandfather)

Figure 20 Audrey's first cousins

Figure 21 Myvanwy Wood

Figure 22 Audrey's relatives

Figure 23 Rhiannon, Myvanwy, Grandpa Wood, and Margaret Louisa

Figure 24 Country Wedding with Audrey's relatives

About the Author

Audrey A. Duncan was born in the mountains of North Wales during the height of World War II. Although the war raged in the valleys below and caused massive destruction, life on a sheep farm in the mountains was relatively calm and happy as children adapted to their changing world.